Captain Drake's Orders

by
Karen Wallace

Illustrations by Martin Remphry

W
FRANKLIN WATTS
LONDON • NEW YORK • SYDNEY

To Jack Hextall

1

Dear Diary

Bobby Cavendish rummaged in his sea chest and pulled out the tiny leather-bound diary his grandmother had given him last Christmas.

"Mind you write in it every day, lad," she had muttered.

"The soothsayers promise t'will be a year like none other."

That had been more than six months ago and Bobby remembered trying to hide a smile as his grandmother waved her arms in the air and shouted words like *calamity, chaos, catastrophe.*

Now in a dark corner in the crew's quarters on the good ship *Revenge*, Bobby wished he had paid more attention to his grandmother's ravings.

Because the soothsayers had been right. England was facing a terrifying invasion by the Spanish Armada. Indeed, men said it was the biggest fleet of ships ever mounted by one country against another.

Bobby opened his diary and uncorked his precious bottle of ink. He picked up a ragged quill pen and wrote:

July 30th 1588. On this day, our captain, Sir Francis Drake, did battle with the Spaniards. We chased 'em. We fired our cannons but we stayed at a distance for fear of being overrun and boarded.

The Spanish galleons are giants in the water. Our own ship is tiny by comparison. It seemed the day would end with nothing gained. Then –

"Bobby Cavendish!" bellowed the first mate, a weasel who called himself Dancin' Jack. "On deck! Captain's orders!"

Bobby's heart went *THUMP!* in his chest. What on earth did Captain Drake

want with him? He slammed his diary shut
and pushed it to the bottom of the chest.
Then he pulled on the new jerkin his
grandmother had given him when he
joined the ship's company.

As he ran through the galley, George
Flubbins, the cook, shoved a lump of
bread into his hand. "Eat it," he muttered.
"I 'ears you ain't coming back
for a while."

Bobby's
face went as
white as the
scum on top
of George's
sour beer.
"What?
Why not?
What have I
done wrong?"

"Nowt, lad," replied George. "T'is your grandmother's doing."

"My grandmother!" cried Bobby. "What's she got to do with it?"

George rubbed a stinking wet cloth down the front of Bobby's jerkin. "She married a Spanish sailor, din't she?"

Bobby nodded.

"And you speaks Spanish, don'tya?"

"A bit."

"A bit's enough," replied George grimly. "That's what Captain Drake said, when Spooner told 'im."

Bobby's face went purple with fury.

Kit Spooner was the captain's cabin boy and he was *supposed* to be Bobby's friend. Now Captain Drake might think Bobby was a spy. "How dare he –"

"Shut up, lad," said George. "Drake's secretary is sick with the shivers. Kit's done you a favour."

"How do you know?" asked Bobby suspiciously.

"You'll find out," said George, as he pushed Bobby halfway up the ladder. "An' mind yer manners with the captain."

Bobby stumbled onto the lower deck and ran past the great cannons that gleamed dully in the moonlight. It was past midnight and groups of exhausted sailors lay in heaps on the dirty wooden boards. Some had bandages wrapped around their wounds. Bobby tried not to look at the dark red stains.

Suddenly his stomach filled with butterflies!

Where were the other English ships? Only a few hours ago Captain Drake had agreed to stand watch for the fleet and a lantern had been lit on the stern of the *Revenge*. Now that lantern was gone and she was on her own sailing under full sail.

Bobby turned to a sailor who was
wiping down one of the smaller guns with
a greasy cloth. "Where are we?" he asked.
"I thought –"

"I ain't paid to ask questions," muttered
the sailor. He slapped the cloth against the
muzzle of the gun. "And if you've got any
sense, you won't ask 'em, either."

At that moment, Dancin' Jack appeared on deck holding a lantern above his head.

In the smoky yellow light, he looked like some fiendish goblin. "I bin looking for you everywhere," he snarled, grabbing Bobby by the ear.

Then he dragged him along the deck towards the great cabin where Captain Drake had his quarters.

2

A Bit is Enough

"I don't recall giving you orders to twist this boy's ears off," said a deep voice above them.

Dancin' Jack let go his grip on Bobby's ears. "Aye, aye, Cap'n Drake, sir," he muttered. "So you didn't, sir."

In the shaft of light that poured from the captain's cabin, Bobby saw a stocky man step forward.

"Indeed, this boy's ears are particularly useful to me."

"Beg your pardon, sir," wheedled Dancin' Jack. "No harm meant, sir."

Even though it was dark, Bobby could sense Drake was smiling. It gave him just enough courage to speak.

"C-C-Captain Drake?" he stammered.

"Don't be afraid, boy," replied Captain Drake, kindly. "Come. I would speak with you, immediately."

The next moment Bobby found himself staring into the bright blue eyes and red-bearded face of the man people said was the finest sailor in all England.

Captain Drake put out his hand. It was a firm friendly handshake and it

helped to stop
Bobby's knees
knocking
inside his
breeches.

"Sit yourself
down, lad,"
said Drake.
Bobby's eyes
took in the
panelled walls
and the long
oak table
covered in charts. On the floor beside it
stood a huge leather-bound sea chest
bulging with scrolls, each one stamped
with a red wax seal.

Captain Drake followed his gaze and
smiled wearily. "My orders," he said.
"Not quite what I'm following right now,

but sometimes a man's instinct is worth a bucket full of orders."

"Yessir," replied Bobby, not understanding a word the captain was saying.

Suddenly Drake's face changed as if the time for idle chatter was over. "You will remember we were guarding the fleet," he said abruptly.

Bobby nodded.

"You will see we are no longer."

Bobby nodded.

Drake walked to the window and peered into the gloom. "We have come across the *Rosario*, a fine fighting galleon of the Spanish Armada. Tomorrow, I plan to board her."

Bobby's eyes went huge and round.

"She is an easy prize, lad," said Drake.
"Her foremast is broken and her sails lie in a
tangle on her deck." He smiled mischievously.
"We do her a favour, I assure you."

Bobby blushed. He knew that the
Spaniards saw Drake as an evil pirate.

"The captain of the *Rosario* is one
Don Pedro des Valdes," continued Drake.
"A man with many secrets, I am sure."

Drake turned from the window and gave an innocent shrug. "The only problem is, my secretary's sick and I don't speak much Spanish." He fixed his blue eyes on Bobby. "Unlike you, lad."

Bobby could feel the colour draining from his face. Inside his breeches his knees began to knock again. "I'll do my best, sir," he whispered. "But I only speak a bit."

"A bit is enough," replied Drake, softly. "Now go and get your sea chest. You will be sleeping in my quarters for the next while."

Bobby's heart leapt in his chest. The captain's quarters were the best on the ship. You got the pickings of the supper table, too. Kit had done him a favour, after all!

Drake rang a small bronze bell. A moment later a bright-eyed boy with a mop of curly black hair came into the room.

Kit Spooner grinned and Bobby grinned back.

"Excellent," cried Drake. "I see you two are already acquainted. Kit, make your friend comfortable tonight. He'll have a busy day of it, tomorrow."

3

Best Beef and Onions

The next morning Bobby Cavendish and Kit Spooner pressed their noses to the tiny leaded windows of the captain's cabin. A gigantic castle of a galleon loomed above them.

Sailors swarmed everywhere. They ran

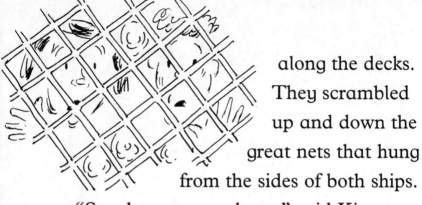

along the decks.
They scrambled
up and down the
great nets that hung
from the sides of both ships.

"See those canvas bags," said Kit
pointing to the heavily loaded rowing boats
going back and forth in the channel of water
between the two ships. "They're full of gold
ducats, they are. Fifty thousand of 'em.

Imagine having all that money."

Bobby stared at the bags. He couldn't imagine what it would be like to own one gold ducat, let alone fifty thousand of them. No wonder Sir Francis Drake had been so keen to 'rescue' the *Rosario*!

Bobby walked out onto the small deck in front of the captain's cabin. The air was full of voices shouting in Spanish, but more than anything it was full of the stink of rotten fish.

"Ugh!" said Kit, coming up beside him. "I've heard Spanish rations were bad," he wrinkled his nose, "but not *this* bad."

"Cook says they only get fish and rice with a bit of wine, and that's mostly vinegar," replied Bobby. "No beef and no beer."

"Poor blighters," muttered Kit.

There were more men on the *Rosario* than Bobby had even seen in his life. Most of them looked like soldiers rather than sailors or gunners. Now they stood in unhappy groups, their muskets thrown in huge piles in the middle of the deck.

"Look!" cried Kit. "There's the captain! Standing by that cannon!"

Bobby's eyes travelled along the row of

heavy two-wheeled cannons that lined the deck of the *Rosario*. Sure enough, there was Drake with one of his officers.

"What do you think they're talking about?" asked Bobby, his heart thumping in his chest. As he spoke he tried to remember the Spanish word for gun or cannon or ammunition. He couldn't think of any!

Kit shrugged. "I've heard our sailors say those Spanish ships are too big to beat." He grinned. "I bet our captain's looking for a way to beat 'em."

At that moment a trumpet sounded.

A man in a richly quilted doublet wearing a high round hat stuck with feathers walked slowly down the centre of the galleon. A long sword with a gold and silver hilt hung from his side.

That must be Don Pedro des Valdes, the captain of the *Rosario*, thought Bobby.

His stomach turned into a bag of ice. Soon he would be sitting in the captain's cabin, translating Don Pedro's words into English!

The two men bowed.

Then Sir Francis Drake turned and they walked together towards the nets. An empty rowing boat waited on the water below.

◆

It was well after midnight when Bobby opened his sea chest and pulled out his diary.

July 31st. My Spanish is better than I thought! Grandma would be proud of me!

At first Don Pedro refused to surrender.
Then the captain said he would take the
ship, anyway. He even offered to keep Don
Pedro hostage at his own house in Devon!
Then Don Pedro wouldn't speak (which
was lucky for me!). All I could hear was his
stomach rumbling. Then I had a brilliant
idea. Grandma used to say a Spaniard
thinks with his stomach. When I told the
captain, he grinned from ear to ear. Next
thing we were all tucking into cook's best
beef and onions, washed down with beer.

Then Don Pedro smacked his lips and begin to talk. Kit was right about the guns. The Spanish use two-wheeled cannons and Don Pedro says they are very heavy to move. He also says that all their ships are trying to meet up with Spanish soldiers who are marching down from Holland. Anyway, I remembered just about all the words and Captain Drake wrote everything in a little book.

Bobby yawned. He was exhausted! It had been the busiest and the most important day of his life. He rolled out a straw mattress and fell into a deep sleep.

4

Fire! Fire!

Five days later as Bobby Cavendish carried water to wounded sailors lying anywhere they could find shelter, he remembered that night on the mattress. It was the last decent meal and the last decent sleep he had had on board the *Revenge*.

The next day, the *Revenge* had returned to the English fleet and Don Pedro was taken ashore as hostage. Drake had immediately gone to talks with the other English captains. And next thing everyone knew, the fleet was divided into four squadrons, rather than the whole fleet operating as one huge force. This meant each captain could be given a separate task and attacks could be planned more accurately.

This new state of affairs suited Captain Drake who immediately sailed out to sea leaving the other groups to fight the Spanish fleet near the coast.

At first the crew of the *Revenge* didn't understand what was happening. It looked as if they were off on another of Drake's so-called 'rescue' missions.

But Drake knew what he was doing.

"The wind will change, lads," he cried. "Mark my words. Then when we're at sea, we'll turn and creep up on those Spaniards from behind!"

Which is exactly what happened.

Bobby leant against a cannon, suddenly feeling weak at the memory.

"It was bad, wasn't it?" said a voice beside him. "All that fire and screaming." Kit Spooner put down his bucket and sat next to him. "Dancin' Jack won't be dancing no more, either."

"Oh," said Bobby in a numb voice. "I'm sorry about that."

"I ain't," muttered Kit. "He twisted my ears so hard, I thought they'd fall off one of these days." He reached into his pocket. "Here, George gave me this for you."

It was a hunk of mouldy cheese but it was food. As Bobby chewed, he began to feel better. "We chased them Spaniards away, didn't we, Kit?"

he said suddenly with a grin.

"All the way to
Calais in France,
I've heard," replied
Kit, reaching for his
own piece of cheese.
He leaned over and
whispered in Kit's
ear. "Captain
says there's going
be a big meeting on
the *Ark Royal*."

"Whose ship's that?" asked Bobby who
could never remember who was captain
of which ship.

"That's Lord Admiral Howard's ship,"
said Kit through a mouthful of cheese.
"He's making Cap'n Frobisher and Cap'n
Hawkins, Sirs, just like our captain is."

"Oh." Bobby thought for a bit.

"Does that mean we get a decent night's sleep for a change?"

Kit laughed. "It certainly does, an' we'll be the first to hear the new plans when they get back." He winked. "Sir Francis Drake always brings out the brandy and tongues start wagging like tails on billy goats."

◆

Two days later, Bobby finally found the time to write in his diary.

August 7th. We're going to try and set fire to the Armada.

It was Captain Drake's idea! You fill up some old ships with tar and pitch and anything that will burn, and load the guns with double the shot. A hundred men have volunteered to sail them into the harbour at Calais. (They jump ship at the last moment, Kit says!) Everything has to be done quickly because the wind and the tide are just right.

Captain Drake has already started work on one of his ships and –

At that moment a drumbeat pounded the air. It was a signal that Sir Francis Drake wanted to speak to his crew.

Bobby stuffed his diary into his sea chest and scrambled on deck as fast as he could.

The stocky figure strode backwards and forwards on the deck outside his cabin waving his hands as he spoke.

"Eight ships are on their way," he shouted.

There was a gasp of astonishment.
Eight ships in so short a time! It was
nothing short of a miracle.

"They set sail on the evening tide and

with God's will, they will rid us once and for all of this Spanish *Armada*." He spat out the last word as if it was a piece of rotten meat.

Then everyone looked out to sea and a huge roar went up from the crew.

Bobby turned. What he saw then, he knew he would never forget.

Lashed together, their prows streaming fire, eight ships appeared out of the night on their way towards the port of Calais and the heart of the Spanish Armada!

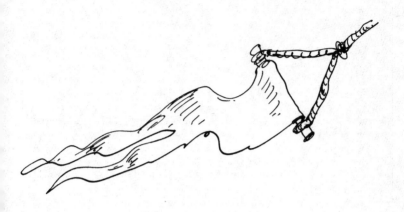

5

The Wind Blows North!

When the battle began the next day,
Bobby Cavendish realized that what he
had known before had been nothing more
than skirmishes.

The fireships had not managed to
destroy the Armada but they had done the

next best thing. The great Spanish fleet
had cut their anchors and fled in different
directions. Now the English ships could
take on the small groups that were left and
this time they did not keep their distance.

The *Revenge*, like Captain Frobisher's
Triumph and Lord Admiral Howard's

Ark Royal, dodged in and out the huge
clumsy galleons like terriers.

"You can see their faces!" shouted
Bobby as he handed Kit a bucket of water.

Kit opened his mouth to reply but a
huge *BANG!* from the cannon behind
exploded into the air. Kit threw himself at

Bobby's stomach and pulled him to
the ground.

A spatter of gunshot hit the mast
where Bobby had been standing!

Now it was Bobby's turn to try and
speak. But the air was full of choking
black smoke from the burning powder.

"More water!" shouted Kit and pushed
him back down the deck.

Bobby stumbled towards the huge
water butt in the middle of the ship, his

canvas bucket banging at his legs.

All around men swore and screamed as they fought to reload the cannons and swing them round to aim a better shot.

Bobby watched in amazement as two Spanish seamen struggled in the water. At first he thought they had been thrown overboard, then he saw them jamming rope and tar into the side of their ship to stop it from sinking.

It was a brave thing to do, even if they were Spanish!

"You!" yelled an officer, grabbing Bobby roughly by the shoulder. It was the same man he had seen with Captain Drake beside the cannon on board the *Rosario*.

"Find the Captain! Tell him we're running low on ammunition!" Bobby dropped his bucket and clambered up the ladder onto the next deck.

Through the smoke, he could see
Drake running from one side of the ship to
the other, shouting orders. Thick sweat
dripped down his face and there was blood
on his arm.

At that moment, the *Revenge* lurched
in the water. Sails cracked and the ship
changed course.

Within minutes the gunners had
reloaded the cannons and were firing from

the other side. Bobby thought of the two-wheeled guns he had seen on the *Rosario*. He remembered Don Pedro explaining how heavy they were and almost impossible to move.

No wonder Captain Drake had decided to fight at close range. The Spanish guns could never be turned around fast enough to get a good aim at the English ships!

Bobby ran up to him and screamed his message above the roar of the guns but Drake was looking up at a tiny flag fluttering from the top mast and didn't seem to hear him.

Bobby was just about to shout again when Drake's face broke into a tiger's grin.

"See, boy!" he cried to Bobby as he pointed upwards.

Bobby looked up at the tiny fluttering flag.

"The wind blows north, boy! They'll be
driven onto the sandbanks," shouted
Drake, his voice hoarse with excitement.
"The day is ours!"

Bobby stared at the ships tossing and turning in the choppy water. Everywhere was smoke and fire and confusion.

How could Drake say the battle was over?

Yet hours later when the wind changed again scattering the Armada and blowing it into the North Sea, Bobby remembered this moment.

The captain had been absolutely right!

6

Good Wages

Two weeks later, Bobby Cavendish crept
along the passageway towards the crew's
quarters that were his once more. All
around him, sailors were roaring and
swearing. Only now they were dancing
and laughing, too!

Beer and brandy flowed through the boat like a swollen river after a rainstorm. Ever since the battle was over, the *Revenge* and her crew had been celebrating.

Bobby didn't like the taste of beer and he had promised his grandmother not to drink brandy until he was twenty-one. As for dancing, the last sailor he bumped into had picked him up and spun him round as if he was a doll!

It was more frightening than all the battles put together!

Bobby crept into his corner and pulled out his diary from the bottom of his sea chest. He uncorked the tiny bottle of ink. There was hardly any left. Then he dipped in his ragged quill pen and wrote:

August 19th. The wind that blew away the Spanish fleet still blows. They are being pushed north towards Scotland.

Our captain wants to give chase but Queen Elizabeth says no and the captain must obey her orders. Kit is to be promoted to first cabin boy! I don't know what is to happen to me. I had hoped –

"Bobby!" cried Kit's voice from the end of the passageway. He sounded breathless and excited. "Hurry! The captain wants you!"

Bobby quickly hid his diary in his sea chest. Then he pulled on the jerkin that grandmother had given him. It was ripped and torn now and some of the stains were brownish red.

Kit's face appeared in front of him. There was a big white grin in his grimy face.

"What is it?" cried Bobby, climbing like

a monkey up the ladder to the deck.

"It's brilliant, that's what it is!" cried Kit. And with that he pulled open the captain's cabin and pushed Bobby inside.

Sir Francis Drake was sitting behind his long oak table. There was a cut across his forehead that looked sore but below his blue eyes were quick and bright.

"Sit down, lad," he said. "I have a proposition for you."

All sorts of possibilities ran through Bobby's head. Did the captain need another cabin boy? Did he know of another captain who needed a cabin boy?

"I owe you great thanks, Bobby," said Drake. "That night we took the *Rosario*, I learned much." He paused. "Indeed, I would wager that your 'bit' of Spanish helped defeat the Armada!"

Bobby felt the colour drain from his face. He felt the room begin to spin. He stared as hard as he could at the bronze bell on the table to stop himself from falling off his chair in a faint.

"Thank you, sir," he whispered. "T'is all my grandma's doing."

"For which England is grateful, lad," replied Drake smiling. He walked around the table and put his hand on Bobby's shoulder.

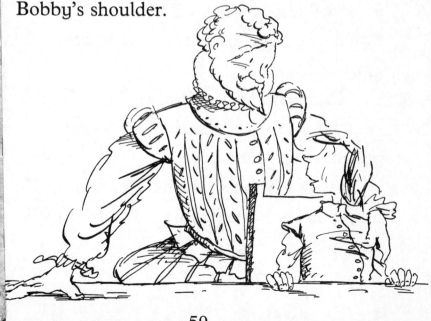

"As you know, Kit will become my first cabin boy but I want *you* to join my household as my own secretary."

This was just about the last thing Bobby had expected. "But I'm not good enough," he spluttered.

"You will learn as part of your duties," replied Drake. "I've plans to buy a house on the Thames." He winked. "Would that suit you?"

Bobby could only nod his head! Never in his wildest dreams did he ever think he would even *see* London, let alone live in it!

"Excellent!" cried Drake. Then he reached into his breeches' pocket and pulled out a round gold coin.

It was a Spanish ducat. One of the fifty thousand ducats taken off the *Rosario* that night.

"Wages," said Drake, putting the ducat into Bobby's hand. "Good wages for a job well done."

Bobby stared at the coin in his hand and shook his head. A whole gold ducat. It was a fortune. He couldn't possibly have earned it. "I-I –" he stammered.

Drake laughed. "I-I, couldn't have done without you, lad," he said "Take it. Captain's orders."

Notes

Why war?

Philip II of Spain wanted to make England a Catholic country again. He wanted to stop English sailors like Drake raiding Spanish ships off South America and stealing their gold. He also wanted to take revenge on Elizabeth I for helping the Dutch with their war against Spain.

The Spanish Armada

One hundred and thirty ships made up the Armada. Half of them were galleons, merchant ships and armed galleys. The others were ships carrying stores and extra ammunition. About thirty thousand men joined up. Most of them were soldiers with little or no knowledge of the sea.

The English fleet

The English had one hundred and ninety-seven ships. The ships were smaller than the Spanish ships, but much faster in the water. Only sixteen thousand men joined up but almost all of them were proper sailors and knew the waters well.

Guns and gunners

Spanish guns had two wheels and were clumsy and difficult to reload. English guns had four wheels and so could be moved and aimed more easily. The English also had special gunners who practised reloading quickly.

What's on the menu?

Meals at sea were
pretty terrible
and both crews
suffered from food
poisoning. Spanish
crews were fed on fish, oil, rice and wine. The
English had beef, butter and beer. Both crews ate
bacon, cheese and biscuits. However, the Spanish
ration per day was much less than the English
and their fish went bad very quickly.

The defeat of the Armada

Although the last battle helped to defeat the
Armada, the English were lucky that the wind
changed and blew the Spanish ships north. The
Armada then had to sail around Scotland and
Ireland to get home.

English war medals were engraved
with the inscription: 'God
breathed and they were scattered.'